SULTANA RAZIA

SULTANA RAZIA WAS THE ONLY REIGNING QUEEN WHO EVER SAT ON THE THRONE OF DELHI. SHE WAS THE DAUGHTER OF SULTAN SHAMSUDDIN ILTUTMISH OF THE SLAVE DYNASTY.

IN 1236, SULTAN ILTUTMISH RETURNED TO DELHI WITH HIS VICTORIOUS TROOPS AFTER CRUSHING A REBELLION IN SIND.

WELCOME HOME, MY LORD. I TRUST ALL WENT WELL.

VICTORY WAS OURS. BUT IT WAS A TIRING CAMPAIGN.

IT MUST HAVE BEEN. YOU LOOK ILL, MY LORD! LET ME SUMMON THE DOCTOR.

LATER, SHAH TURKAN. THERE ARE MORE PRESSING MATTERS THAT NEED ATTENTION. SEND FOR TAJUDDIN.

TAJUDDIN WAS HIS TRUSTED MINISTER.

TAJUDDIN, I HAVE DECIDED TO MAKE RAZIA, MY SUCCESSOR.

MAKE A WILL BUT KEEP ITS CONTENTS A SECRET. READ IT TO THE DURBAR ONLY AFTER MY DEATH.

YES, YOUR MAJESTY.

FORGIVE ME, MY IMPERTINENCE, MY LORD. WHAT ABOUT RUKNUDDIN. AND GHIASUDDIN, OUR SONS?

THEY ARE DEVOTED TO THE PLEASURES OF YOUTH, MY MALIKA. I DARE NOT ENTRUST THE KINGDOM TO THEM.

ON APRIL 29, 1236, ILTUTMISH, THE GREATEST OF THE SLAVE KINGS, DIED.

THE SULTAN IS DEAD!

AFTER THE FUNERAL, TAJUDDIN SUMMONED THE FORTY AMIRS *AND READ OUT THE SULTAN'S WILL.

THE NIZAM-UL-MULK** WAS THE FIRST TO VOICE THE FEELINGS OF THE ANGRY AMIRS.

HOW COULD HIS MAJESTY DO SUCH A THING?

HOW CAN WE SWEAR ALLEGIANCE TO A WOMAN?

THE PRINCESS MAY PROVE TO BE AN EFFICIENT RULER, AYAZ. HAVE YOU FORGOTTEN WHAT AN EXCELLENT ADMINISTRATOR SHE MADE WHEN THE SULTAN WAS AWAY AT GWALIOR?

* POWERFUL TURKISH NOBLES   4   ** PRIME MINISTER

AMIR ALTUNIA, WE KNOW YOU ARE FOND OF THE PRINCESS. BUT···

MY GOOD FRIENDS, PLEASE STOP QUARRELLING. I UNDERSTAND YOUR PREJUDICE AGAINST MY SEX. THEREFORE, LET US ALL SWEAR ALLEGIANCE TO MY BROTHER, RUKNUDDIN.

I HEREBY PROCLAIM YAMIN-UD-DAULAH RUKNUDDIN THE SULTAN OF DELHI.

LONG LIVE SULTAN RUKNUDDIN!

LATER—

WHY DID YOU SURRENDER, NOBLE PRINCESS?

YOU LOVE ME ALTUNIA, SO YOU ARE BLIND TO THE PREJUDICES OF MEN AGAINST WOMEN AND WANT ME TO BE QUEEN.

THAT MAY BE TRUE. BUT THERE ARE MANY OTHERS READY TO SUPPORT YOU.

YOU ARE KIND. YET WE MUST NOT BE HASTY. IF IT IS ALLAH'S WILL THAT I SHOULD BE THE SULTANA, NO MAN CAN PREVENT IT.

BUT LET US AT LEAST BE PREPARED FOR ANY PLOT SHAH TURKAN MAY HATCH! I DO NOT TRUST THAT WOMAN.

YOU ARE RIGHT ALTUNIA, BUT WE SHOULD NOT LET IT WORRY US.

AS ILTUTMISH HAD FORESEEN, RUKNUDDIN LED A LIFE OF PLEASURE, NEGLECTING THE AFFAIRS OF STATE.

THE GOVERNORS OF LAHORE AND HANSI WOULD LIKE AN AUDIENCE WITH YOUR MAJESTY.

TELL THEM I AM BUSY. I HAVE NO TIME TO MEET THEM.

WHY DON'T YOU MEET THEM, YOUR MAJESTY? I BESEECH YOU TO DEVOTE MORE TIME TO STATE AFFAIRS.

AND I BESEECH YOU NOT TO BE IRKSOME.

MEANWHILE, SHAH TURKAN GREW JEALOUS OF HER STEP-DAUGHTER, RAZIA'S INCREAS-ING POPULARITY WITH THE SUBJECTS.

I MUST GET RID OF RAZIA.

ONE DARK NIGHT, AS JAMAL-UD-DIN YAQUT, THE KEEPER OF THE ROYAL STABLES, WAS WALKING HURRIEDLY TOWARDS THE PALACE—

HOW CARELESS OF ME TO HAVE FORGOTTEN TO TIE THE PRINCESS' HORSE...

HEY! WHAT ARE THOSE MEN UP TO?

WHY, THEY ARE DIGGING A PIT! RIGHT WHERE THE PRINCESS EXERCISES HER HORSE EVERY DAY!

AND THEY ARE COVERING IT! A CAMOUFLAGE!

IT'S A PLOT TO KILL HER! I MUST WARN THE PRINCESS!

A THOUSAND PARDONS, YOUR HIGHNESS, BUT I MUST SPEAK TO YOU AT ONCE!

AT THIS HOUR, YAQUT? CAN'T IT WAIT TILL MORNING?

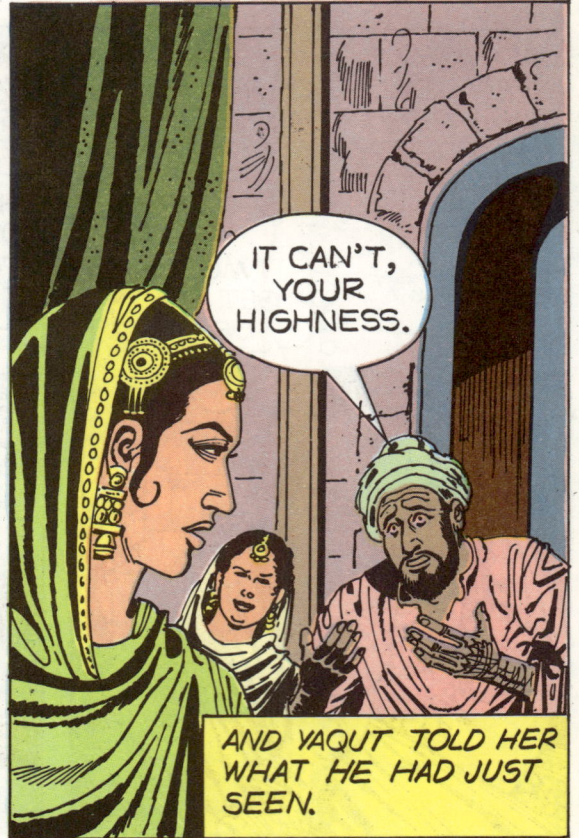

IT CAN'T, YOUR HIGHNESS.

AND YAQUT TOLD HER WHAT HE HAD JUST SEEN.

IT IS SHAH TURKAN! SHE WANTS TO GET RID OF ME!

WE MUST EXPOSE HER, YOUR HIGHNESS.

YES, YAQUT. SUMMON TAJUDDIN AND ALTUNIA.

THE NEXT MORNING, DELHI WAS FULL OF WILD RUMOURS.

THOUSANDS OF EXCITED PEOPLE RUSHED TO THE RIDING GROUND EXPECTING TO WITNESS THEY KNEW NOT WHAT.

HERE COMES THE PRINCESS!

WHAT A SPLENDID HORSEWOMAN SHE IS!

BUT AS THE HORSE WAS ABOUT TO JUMP THE FENCE, RAZIA SUDDENLY REINED HIM IN AND TURNED TO NIZAM-UL-MULK—

I REQUEST YOU TO EXAMINE THAT SPOT.

A STRANGE REQUEST! BUT THE PRINCESS MUST HAVE HER REASONS.

AND HE WALKED TO THE SPOT.

10

IT IS THE HAND OF SHAH TURKAN!

SEIZE HER!

MURDERESS!

JUST THEN SULTAN RUKNUDDIN APPEARED.

WHY THIS COMMOTION?

THE QUEEN MOTHER HIRED THESE MEN TO KILL ME. I BESEECH YOU, THE SULTAN, THAT THE GUILTY BE PUNISHED.

THE QUEEN MOTHER PLOTTING TO KILL YOU? IMPOSSIBLE! I'LL HAVE YOU PUT TO DEATH FOR PLOTTING AGAINST ME!

NO! NO!

PUNISH SHAH TURKAN!

SEIZE THE SULTAN!

KILL! KILL!

SUDDENLY, A SAINTLY FIGURE CAME FORWARD.

IT IS SAINT KAZIMUDDIN ZAHID!

I DEMAND IN THE NAME OF THE AMIRS, THE SOLDIERS AND THE PEOPLE, THE DEPOSITION OF SULTAN RUKNUDDIN AND THE INSTALLATION OF THE NOBLE LADY SULTANA RAZIA, AS OUR NEW RULER.

LONG LIVE SULTANA RAZIA!

MY PEOPLE! I PROMISE BEFORE GOD THAT I SHALL PROVE WORTHY OF YOUR TRUST. AND BECAUSE I AM BORN A WOMAN, I HERE AND NOW SOLEMNLY PLEDGE THAT I SHALL SIT ON THIS GREAT THRONE OF OUR ANCESTORS ONLY IF I PROVE TO BE AS GOOD AS ANY MAN.

LONG LIVE THE SULTANA!

RAZIA DRESSED AND ACTED LIKE A KING. SHE HAD COINS STRUCK IN HER NAME···

···AND HELD CONSULTATIONS WITH THE FORTY AMIRS.

13

SHE WAS THE LEADER OF HER ARMIES.

SHE RESTORED PEACE AND ORDER IN HER KINGDOM.

SHE BUILT ROADS, PLANTED TREES...

...DUG WELLS...

...ENCOURAGED TRADE...

...DISPENSED JUSTICE...

...ESTABLISHED SCHOOLS, ACADEMIES, PUBLIC LIBRARIES AND...

...PATRONISED SCHOLARS, POETS, PAINTERS AND MUSICIANS

RAZIA APPEARED FREQUENTLY IN PUBLIC WITHOUT A VEIL.

YOUR MAJESTY, IN YOUR ILLUSTRIOUS FATHER'S TIME, YOU NEVER APPEARED THUS BEFORE THE PUBLIC. A THIN VEIL ALWAYS COVERED YOUR NOBLE FACE.

BUT IN MY FATHER'S TIME I WAS NOT THE RULER. NOW I FACE MY SUBJECTS AS THEIR SULTANA.

TRUE, YOUR MAJESTY, BUT YOU ARE A WOMAN...

TO THE PEOPLE, I AM THEIR PROTECTOR AND BENEFACTOR.

YOUR REASONS ARE STRONG, YOUR MAJESTY. BUT TONGUES WAG...

THEN STAY THEM! TELL THE AMIRS THAT MY BEHAVIOUR IS A PART OF MY FAITH.

JUST AS THE NIZAM-UL-MULK LEFT, ALTUNIA ARRIVED.

HERE COMES AN-OTHER MAN! ALTUNIA, ARE YOU ALSO PREJUDICED AGAINST ME BECAUSE I AM A WOMAN?

HOW CAN I BE? I LOVE YOU!

I AM SORRY, ALTUNIA. YOU HAVE ALWAYS BEEN A LOYAL FRIEND AND I LOVE YOU TOO...

...BUT EVER SINCE I HAVE BECOME QUEEN, I AM DISTURBED BY THE ATTITUDE OF MY AMIRS.

HAS SOMEBODY BEEN POISONING YOUR MIND AGAINST ME?

NO ONE CAN DO THAT. WE HAVE BEEN SUCH GOOD FRIENDS SINCE CHILDHOOD. HOW I WISH MY OTHER AMIRS WERE LIKE YOU!

ONE DAY, AT COURT—

I FEEL, THE JAZIAH * SHOULD BE ABOLISHED.

YOUR MAJESTY, THE ABOLITION OF JAZIAH WILL WEAKEN OUR AUTHORITY.

BESIDES, THE TAX IS A REMINDER TO OUR HINDU SUBJECTS THAT WE ARE THEIR RULERS.

MUST WE FORCE SUCH HUMILIATION ON THEM?

IT HAS CONVERTED MANY TO OUR FAITH, BESIDES BEING A SOURCE OF REVENUE, YOUR MAJESTY.

PERHAPS THEY EMBRACED ISLAM OUT OF FEAR.

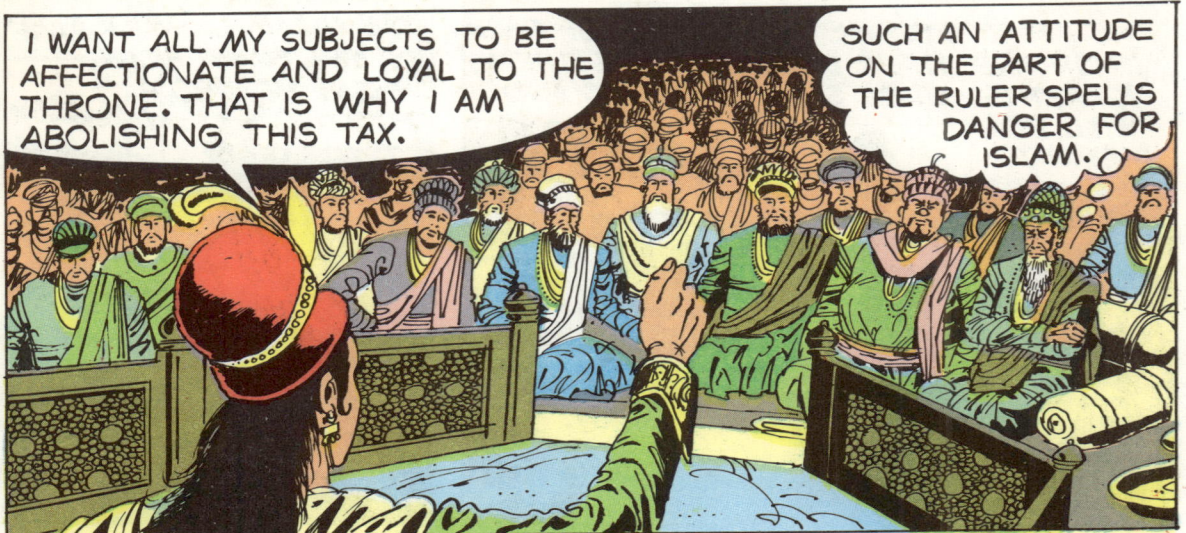

I WANT ALL MY SUBJECTS TO BE AFFECTIONATE AND LOYAL TO THE THRONE. THAT IS WHY I AM ABOLISHING THIS TAX.

SUCH AN ATTITUDE ON THE PART OF THE RULER SPELLS DANGER FOR ISLAM.

* A TAX IMPOSED ON ALL NON-MUSLIMS

SOME OF THE AMIRS LED BY THE NIZAM-UL-MULK PLOTTED TO OVERTHROW RAZIA.

NOW IS THE TIME TO STRIKE!

BUT THE LOYAL ALTUNIA WARNED HER OF IT IN TIME.

YOUR MAJESTY, I MUST WARN YOU! I HAVE HEARD SOME AMIRS ARE PLOTTING AGAINST YOU.

INSTRUCT OUR SPIES TO SPREAD RUMOURS THAT THE NIZAM-UL-MULK IS NEGO-TIATING SECRETLY WITH ME.

THE RUSE WORKED.

DON'T BELIEVE A WORD THAT WILY NIZAM-UL-MULK SAYS AGAINST RAZIA. HE IS REALLY HER STOOGE.

THE AMIRS BECAME SUSPICIOUS OF EACH OTHER AND THEIR DISUNITY MADE THEM WEAK. THEY WERE SOON CAPTURED AND TRIED FOR TREACHERY.

THE NIZAM-UL-MULK FLED TO THE SIMUR HILLS WHERE HE DIED A FUGITIVE.

18

AS A REWARD FOR HIS LOYALTY, RAZIA MADE ALTUNIA THE GOVERNOR OF BHATINDA.

I AM HONOURED, YOUR MAJESTY.

UNDER YOU, AT LEAST THAT PART OF MY EMPIRE WILL BE IN SAFE HANDS.

MARRY ME, RAZIA... BEFORE I LEAVE!

HOW CAN I, ALTUNIA? IT WILL MAKE THE AMIRS JEALOUS.

BUT WHAT ABOUT OUR FEELINGS? WE ARE YOUNG. WE NEED EACH OTHER.

DO YOU THINK I DON'T WANT TO MARRY YOU? BUT FOR THE PRESENT I MUST CONCENTRATE ON THE AFFAIRS OF STATE.

19

SOON AFTER THE DEPARTURE OF ALTUNIA —

FORGIVE US, YOUR MAJESTY, BUT THE AMIRS ARE MUCH UPSET. THEY FEEL YOU HAVE NO CONFIDENCE IN THEM.

THAT IS NONSENSE, BALBAN. I TRUST THEM FULLY.

YOUR MAJESTY, WHAT IS TROUBLING US IS THE APPOINTMENT OF THE ABYSSINIAN JAMAL-UD-DIN YAQUT, AS AMIRUL UMRA.* IS THERE NO TURK WORTHY OF THIS HIGH POST?

OF COURSE, THERE ARE MANY AMONG MY AMIRS. BUT YAQUT IS EQUALLY COMPETENT AND TRUSTWORTHY. HE DESERVES RECOGNITION.

BUT HE IS NOT A TURK...

OUR QURAN SAYS ALL MUSLIMS ARE BROTHERS.

* CHIEF OF NOBLES.

LATER—

WE MUST CHECK HER NOW, OR WE SHALL LOSE ALL POWER.

WE MUST FIND A WAY.

BUT HOW? SHE IS BOTH ABLE AND POPULAR. THE PEOPLE LOVE HER.

MEANWHILE—

YAQUT, SOMETIMES I WONDER WHAT I'D DO WITHOUT YOUR ABLE SUPPORT.

MY LIFE IS AT YOUR COMMAND, NOBLE LADY.

THE AMIRS ARE JEALOUS OF YOU. THEY THINK YOU INFLUENCE MY DECISIONS.

THE AMIRS HATE ME. BUT DO WE HAVE TO PANDER TO THEIR WHIMS? YOUR SUBJECTS LOVE YOU AND WILL BE LOYAL TO YOU.

BUT THE AMIRS ARE THE LEADERS. THAT IS WHY I MUST BE CAREFUL.

OR IS IT BECAUSE YOU LOVE ALTUNIA?

ALTUNIA AND I HAVE AN UNDERSTANDING. EVEN THE AMIRS KNOW THAT ONE DAY WE WILL MARRY.

WHATEVER YOU DECIDE, MY QUEEN, I SHALL REMAIN LOYAL TO YOU.

MEANWHILE AT BHATINDA—

HER MAJESTY OFTEN GOES RIDING WITH THAT ABYSSINIAN INTO THE FOREST.

THE TWO WERE SEEN THE OTHER EVENING LAUGHING AND TALKING NEAR THE LOTUS POOL, YOUR EXCELLENCY.

HOW DARE SHE MAKE A PUBLIC FOOL OF ME! I WILL AVENGE MY HONOUR!

IN DELHI, SOME DAYS LATER—

YOUR MAJESTY, AN URGENT MESSAGE FROM BHATINDA.

I CAN'T BELIEVE IT! ALTUNIA, A TRAITOR!

ASK GENERAL SAIFUDDIN AIBAK AND THE AMIRUL UMRA TO SEE ME IMMEDIATELY.

YES, YOUR MAJESTY.

ON APRIL 3, 1240, IN THE MONTH OF RAMZAN,*THE LONG AND ARDUOUS MARCH TO BHATINDA BEGAN.

AS THE DAYS PASSED, THE HEAT AND THE FASTS TOOK THEIR TOLL OF THE TROOPS.

WEARY AND LOW IN SPIRIT, THEY REACHED BHATINDA TO FIGHT ALTUNIA'S FRESH, WELL-EQUIPPED TROOPS.

* THROUGHOUT THIS MONTH, MUSLIMS FAST FROM DAWN TO DUSK, WITHOUT DRINKING EVEN WATER.

24

THE BATTLE RAGED LONG AND FIERCE. BOTH SIDES FOUGHT BRAVELY.

THE FIERCEST FIGHTING TOOK PLACE WHERE YAQUT WAS COMMANDING THE TROOPS.

YAQUT'S FORCES WERE HOPELESSLY OUTNUMBERED.

DIE, ENEMY OF ALTUNIA!

WITH YAQUT KILLED, RAZIA'S PANIC-STRICKEN TROOPS SURRENDERED.

RAZIA WAS CAPTURED AND MADE A PRISONER OF ALTUNIA, THE MAN WHO HAD DECLARED HE LOVED HER

AT DELHI, ON RAZIA'S DEFEAT, THE FORTY AMIRS PROCLAIMED HER HALF-BROTHER BEHRAM, SULTAN.

AND AT BHATINDA, AS THE WEEKS PASSED, ALTUNIA UNDERSTOOD.

I WAS A JEALOUS FOOL TO HAVE DOUBTED YOUR LOVE! FORGIVE ME, RAZIA.

LET US FORGET THE PAST AND START A NEW LIFE TOGETHER. I LOVE YOU SO!

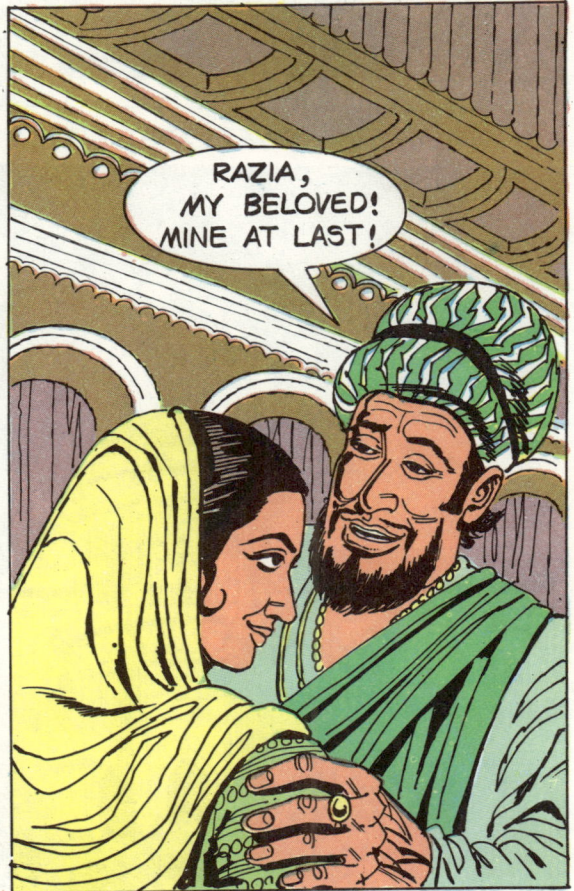

RAZIA, MY BELOVED! MINE AT LAST!

THE WEDDING OF RAZIA AND ALTUNIA WAS CELEBRATED WITH GREAT POMP IN BHATINDA.

AFTER THE BANQUET THAT NIGHT—

SOON, WE SHALL START ON OUR JOURNEY TO TAKE BACK THE THRONE OF DELHI.

A FEW DAYS LATER, THEY RODE FORTH.

WHEN THEY HAD COVERED HALF THE DISTANCE—

SULTAN BEHRAM'S FORCES ARE APPROACHING!

THE BATTLE RAGED FOR HOURS. BOTH SIDES WERE DETERMINED TO DEFEAT THE OTHER.

BUT BEHRAM'S FORCES, MORE IN NUMBER AND BETTER EQUIPPED, GRADUALLY STARTED GAINING OVER THE TROOPS OF RAZIA AND ALTUNIA.

IN THE HEAT OF THE BATTLE, BEHRAM'S EMISSARY APPROACHED ALTUNIA.

SURRENDER, YOUR EXCELLENCY! SULTAN BEHRAM GRANTS YOU FULL PARDON!

I WOULD RATHER DIE FOR RAZIA THAN LIVE FOR THE SULTAN.

ALTUNIA!
ALTUNIA!

A FEW MINUTES LATER, AN ARROW STRUCK RAZIA IN THE HEART AND SHE TOO FELL.

THUS, ON OCTOBER 13, 1240 DIED SULTANA RAZIA OF WHOM THE HISTORIAN FERISHTA WROTE:"SHE HAD NO FAULT BUT THAT SHE WAS A WOMAN."